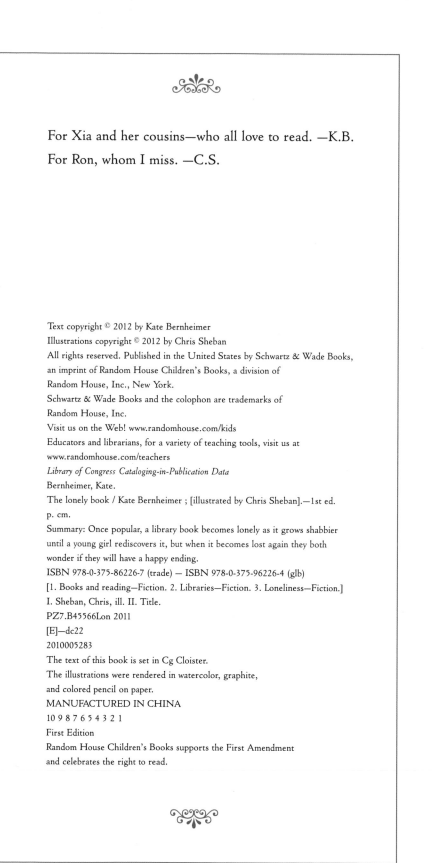

For Xia and her cousins—who all love to read. —K.B.

For Ron, whom I miss. —C.S.

Text copyright © 2012 by Kate Bernheimer
Illustrations copyright © 2012 by Chris Sheban
All rights reserved. Published in the United States by Schwartz & Wade Books,
an imprint of Random House Children's Books, a division of
Random House, Inc., New York.
Schwartz & Wade Books and the colophon are trademarks of
Random House, Inc.
Visit us on the Web! www.randomhouse.com/kids
Educators and librarians, for a variety of teaching tools, visit us at
www.randomhouse.com/teachers
Library of Congress Cataloging-in-Publication Data
Bernheimer, Kate.
The lonely book / Kate Bernheimer ; [illustrated by Chris Sheban].—1st ed.
p. cm.
Summary: Once popular, a library book becomes lonely as it grows shabbier
until a young girl rediscovers it, but when it becomes lost again they both
wonder if they will have a happy ending.
ISBN 978-0-375-86226-7 (trade) — ISBN 978-0-375-96226-4 (glb)
[1. Books and reading—Fiction. 2. Libraries—Fiction. 3. Loneliness—Fiction.]
I. Sheban, Chris, ill. II. Title.
PZ7.B45566Lon 2011
[E]—dc22
2010005283
The text of this book is set in Cg Cloister.
The illustrations were rendered in watercolor, graphite,
and colored pencil on paper.
MANUFACTURED IN CHINA
10 9 8 7 6 5 4 3 2 1
First Edition

The Lonely Book

Kate Bernheimer

illustrated by
Chris Sheban

schwartz & wade books · new york

Once there was a brand-new book that arrived at the library. It was green with a yellow ribbon inside to mark its pages. On its cover was a picture of a girl in the forest under a toadstool. The book found itself in the front of the library where the newest books were always placed.

The library was busy every day with children looking for books about everything in the world, and the moss-green book about the girl in the forest was often chosen and taken home.

Whenever the book was returned, it was placed back on the shelf where the newest books lived. There was a long list of children waiting for the book, and it hardly ever slept at the library.

As is the custom in libraries, after a time the book was moved to the children's section, along with other well-loved books that were no longer new. But the book was still taken home often, and so it was still happy.

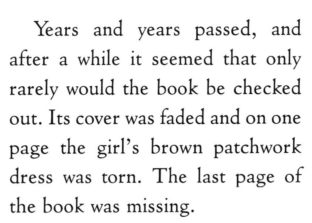

Years and years passed, and after a while it seemed that only rarely would the book be checked out. Its cover was faded and on one page the girl's brown patchwork dress was torn. The last page of the book was missing.

More years passed, and now hardly ever would a child take the shabby book off the shelf. But it was still read with joy from time to time, and despite the book's worn appearance, its girl, toadstool, and story would always be enchanting.

The book became lonely.

Then, one very bad night, the book found itself completely forgotten, dropped in a dark corner by a daydreaming child, and not even the librarian found it.

The next morning, a little girl sat reading in the corner of the library where the book sadly slept. She felt it under the leg of her rocking chair, leaned down, and picked it up. Turning its pages, she sighed.

"Daddy!" she whispered, and walked across to the fairy-tale section. "This is the most beautiful book I've ever read. Can I take it home?"

"I don't know, Alice," her father answered, reading a gigantic book almost bigger than himself. "It seems very fragile. And you already have so many books in your basket."

But Alice put three new books back and so was able to take the lonely book home, promising to be very careful with it.

When the book saw Alice's room—and the shelf where it would sleep, alongside so many familiar books from the library and some new books it had never met—it was very happy.

For six nights in a row, Alice's father read her the book at bedtime, and then after her light was turned out she would read it herself by the light of the moon.

On the last, missing page she always imagined a happy ending and some fairies dancing with the girl around the toadstool.

Now Alice slept with the green book under her pillow, the better to dream about it.

When she went to school every morning, Alice gently tucked the book into her bag. One day, the book was even featured at show-and-tell.

"This is from the library. It's a very old book about a girl and her life under a toadstool," Alice proudly said.

The book had never felt so beloved.

The next week at the library, there was a special event. A princess and a lion greeted Alice and all the children when they arrived and then ushered them into the Listening Room for a wonderful story about a princess and a lion.

After the event, Alice selected the princess and lion storybook to check out. In her excitement, she forgot all about renewing the old book about the girl in the forest.

But as soon as Alice arrived home, she remembered. "Daddy!" she cried. "I left my book at the library. Please can we go back and get it?"

"I'm sorry, Alice," her father replied. "The library is closed now, and I have to work all week. I promise I'll take you back next Saturday morning. I'm sure your friend the book will be there."

The following Saturday, Alice rushed back to the children's section, but the faded green book wasn't there. The librarian looked and looked for it, but she couldn't find it either. (A hardworking library volunteer had picked it up and, thinking it was meant for the Book Sale, taken it down to the basement. There the lonely book sat, patiently waiting for something to happen.)

Alice found a lot of other books to borrow, but they weren't the same. Saturday after Saturday she looked, but her book was never there. Alice missed it terribly.

And the lonely book missed Alice.
Though all the books were kept tidy
and safe in the basement, it was very
dark. The book was lonelier than it
had ever been.

Over time, Alice forgot about the book. Though she never really stopped loving it, it was replaced in her thoughts by other books, like a particularly sweet one about a sea horse and her sea home, and another mysterious one about ice, snow, and glass.

Meanwhile, at the library, volunteers occasionally came down to the basement to tend to the books or bring them new companions. Sometimes a volunteer would pick the lonely book up, leaf through its pages, and smile, remembering its marvelous toadstool. But the volunteer always put it back down with a sigh and left it behind.

The book grew lonelier and lonelier.

Then came a day that the book would remember forever. One morning, it found itself being carried upstairs and placed in the shade of a tree.

The book enjoyed the fresh air. All day long people peered down at it with kind faces, and many children picked it up and turned its pages. Other books were taken away, tucked under people's arms—good books about all sorts of good things, such as faraway planets and talking dogs. Still, none was quite as magical as the lonely book. Neither was any as ruined, which might have been why no one took the lonely book home.

As the sky darkened, it started to rain. Volunteers began to pack up the sale. If someone had looked closely at the lonely book's cover, they would have seen that the girl under the toadstool had started to cry.

It wasn't long before the book heard a familiar voice. "I know it's here, I just know it is. I promise I'll hurry," the voice said breathlessly to the librarian.

"Okay, sweetheart, because we have to get the books out of the rain," the librarian answered.

And then . . . the book found itself in Alice's hands once again. "I knew I'd find you!" Alice cried, gently touching the frayed yellow ribbon.

"Oh, Alice, I've been hoping you'd come!" said the librarian. "The book has been waiting for you. Please, take it for free.

"You know," she added, gazing at the book's cover, with its little girl and enchanted toadstool, "it was my favorite book too when I was young."

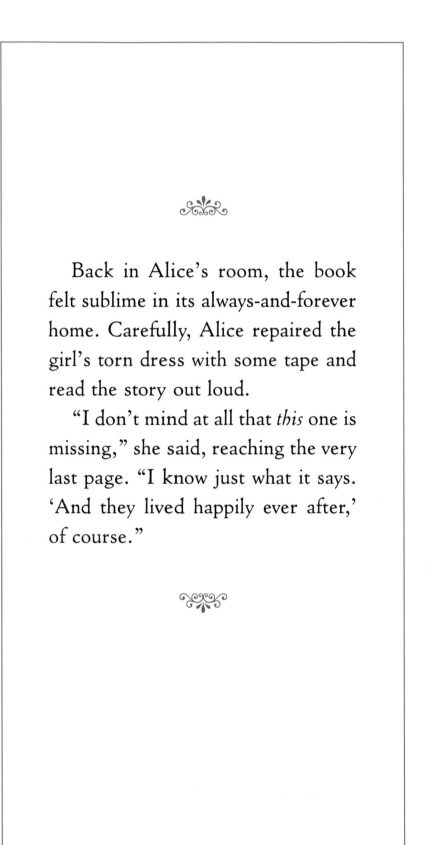

Back in Alice's room, the book felt sublime in its always-and-forever home. Carefully, Alice repaired the girl's torn dress with some tape and read the story out loud.

"I don't mind at all that *this* one is missing," she said, reaching the very last page. "I know just what it says. 'And they lived happily ever after,' of course."